Shakespeare's

Greatest Stories

Abridged and Illustrated

JULIUS CAESAR

Wonder House

Wonder House

(An imprint of Prakash Books)

contact@wonderhousebooks.com

ISBN : 9789389567427

About the Author

William Shakespeare

William Shakespeare is undoubtedly one of the greatest playwrights to have ever lived. He gained fame for his excellent ability to portray human emotions in the form of comedies, tragedies, tragic-comedies and historical plays. Some of his greatest plays include *Macbeth, Hamlet, Romeo and Juliet, The Merchant of Venice, A Midsummer Night's Dream, Julius Caesar, As You Like It, Othello, The Tempest*, and many more. He has been credited with giving the world a plethora of new words and phrases, which are used in our daily language today.

Popularly known as the "Bard of Avon", Shakespeare's contributions to literature are numerous and significant. Apart from plays, he also wrote sonnets and poems. Along with being a writer, Shakespeare was also a co-owner of a theatrical company named Lord Chamberlain's Men. Later, he became a co-owner of The Globe Theatre, which was built in 1599. The Globe is still one of the most cherished theatres in the world and manages to put up thrilling productions of Shakespeare's best works even today.

Cast List

Julius Caesar

Julius Caesar: A Roman General and Senator

Brutus: Caesar's friend, a supporter of the Republic

Antony: Caesar's loyal friend

Cassius: Brutus' friend, a talented General

Octavius: Caesar's adopted son and appointed successor

Casca: A public figure opposing Caesar's rise to power

Calphurnia: Caesar's wife

Portia: Brutus' wife

Flavius: A tribune

Cicero: A Roman senator

Marullus: A tribune who condemns the plebeians

Decius: A member of the conspiracy

Lepidus: Third member of Antony and Octavius's coalition

Of all the wonders that I have heard,
It seems to me most strange that men should fear;
Seeing death, a necessary end,
Will come when it will come.

– **Julius Caesar**, Act I, Scene 2

Julius Caesar, a legendary Roman military general, had expanded his empire by winning a series of epic battles. Loved and respected by all, Caesar rose to become a powerful Roman politician in the succeeding years of his life. He visited the kingdoms of great kings and conquered many foreign lands.

At the pinnacle of his power, the mighty Pompey challenged him to the battle of Pharsalus. Unsurprisingly,

Caesar won the battle and vanquished the Republic, making Pompey flee to Egypt.

Soon, the news of Caesar's triumph over Pompey spread throughout Rome. The commoners left their jobs and crowded the streets of Rome to celebrate Caesar's victory. However, not everyone was happy with Caesar's triumph. Many of Caesar's enemies sent the commoners back to work before the celebrations could even begin.

Two men, Flavius and Marullus, were scolding the carpenters, cobblers, and other commoners to resume their daily jobs. The commoners, in return, regaled the story of Caesar's victory in the battle of Pharsalus. Marullus scolded them, "Are you all mad? You should thank God for sparing you the punishment for such ingratitude! Don't you remember worshipping Pompey? Today you celebrate his defeat! You should be ashamed of yourselves!"

The commoners listened to Marullus quietly and dispersed. "Marullus, we must ensure that no one celebrates Caesar's victory. There should be no decorations for his welcome," said Flavius.

That afternoon, the trumpets announced Caesar's arrival. A large crowd followed Caesar's carriage. Suddenly,

Caesar stopped his carriage and pointed towards his wife who was standing in the crowd.

He addressed Mark Antony, "I shall have Calphurnia stand in your path before the holy race. Make sure you touch her during the race. It is said that if you touch an infertile woman during this race, she's freed of her barrenness."

Antony moved forward and touched Calphurnia. At that moment, a fortune-teller in the crowd called Caesar's name. Caesar asked the fortune-teller what he wanted. He answered, "Sir, beware of the fifteenth of March. It will be the worst day for you."

Caesar ignored his warning and moved ahead with his attendants. Soon, the place emptied, leaving Brutus and Cassius alone.

Cassius asked, "Brutus, do you want to take part in the holy race?"

Brutus shook his head. "No, I am not as competitive as Antony. But you can go to the race!"

Cassius replied, "Don't mind me, but I have noticed that you are less friendly to me nowadays ..."

"No, Cassius, I am just uncomfortable and uneasy. My inner conflicts are troubling me."

Cassius apologised to Brutus for misunderstanding his feelings. He urged him to look within himself and eradicate all sins from there to find some peace. Brutus was confused.

"I will help you in realising your true self, Brutus," said Cassius.

Suddenly, they heard the sound of trumpets.

"What is that commotion?" asked Brutus. "Oh! I am afraid they have crowned Caesar their king!"

"Brutus, do you hate Caesar?" Cassius asked carefully.

"No. I love Caesar very much. Anyway, tell me what did you want to talk about? If it's regarding the goodwill of the Romans, then I will listen. If not, then let me leave." He hurriedly brushed Cassius off.

"I know that you care about the Romans very much. We are similar to Caesar, and we are as free as he is. Once, Caesar challenged me to jump into the rough waters. I didn't think for a moment before jumping, but when I asked Caesar to follow, he jumped and got trapped amidst the harsh waves. I rescued him. Today, he has become ambitious and acts like God. It amuses me to see such a weak man speak so highly of himself in front of the Romans!"

A loud shout interrupted Cassius. More trumpets started playing.

"I think they are applauding for Caesar's new awards," said Brutus.

Cassius replied bitterly, "I wonder what is so special about Caesar? How are his victories any better than yours? You eat the same food as him. There is no difference between you and Caesar, but he is given special treatment all the time."

Brutus realised that perhaps Cassius disliked Caesar. "I believe that you truly care for me, Cassius. I understand what you are trying to tell me. I will think about what you've said and share my thoughts later, but for now, I will hold my tongue."

They abruptly stopped talking when they saw Caesar himself walking towards them, a thunderous expression on his face, with Casca and his followers. Cassius advised Brutus to pull Casca aside and find out what was happening.

When Caesar stopped to discuss something with Antony, Brutus took Casca aside.

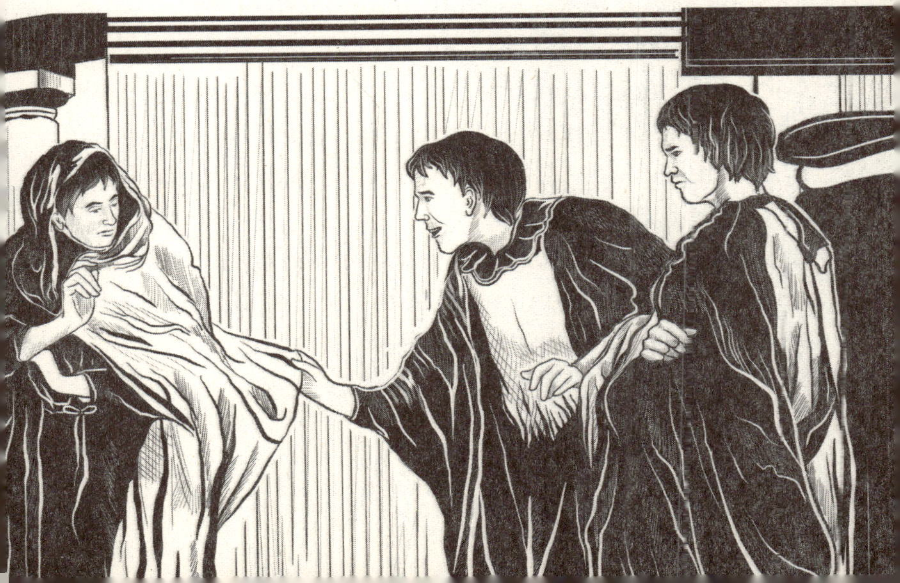

"Casca, tell us what happened today. Why does Caesar look upset?"

Casca told him that the crown was offered to Caesar thrice by Antony, but he declined each time. "The crowd was shouting for this reason. I don't know any more as I felt it was all too silly to pay attention to. I feel that Caesar was just pretending to refuse the crown. The crowd was being so ridiculous! I had to control my laughter!"

Meanwhile, Caesar pointed towards Cassius and said to Antony, "Look at him! How lean and unhealthy! I don't want such men in my country."

Antony replied, "Sir, Cassius is a noble Roman who is completely harmless."

Cassius asked Casca to continue the story. Casca replied, "When Antony offered the crown for the third time, Caesar denied, and everyone screamed. I believe that Caesar couldn't pretend anymore, which is why he had a fit and he collapsed. That's why he looks so serious."

Casca turned to leave but was stopped by Brutus asking him if he wanted to dine with them. He politely declined and bid them goodbye. Brutus left soon after him.

Cassius watched Brutus walking home and smiled, satisfied. "It's so easy to bend Brutus's frame of mind. Caesar hates me but he loves Brutus. And I have influenced Brutus to conspire against Caesar.

Tonight, I will plant some letters inside Brutus's house and make it seem like the citizens have written these letters. In them, I will hint at the possibility of Brutus becoming the king instead of Caesar."

That evening, thunder struck the town. Casca was sipping wine at home with Cicero. He warned Cicero about thunder being a bad omen. Cicero said, "It must be an omen, but I believe that men usually interpret things as per their wishes and circumstances. We tend to forget their real meaning most of the time. Anyway, tell me Casca, does Caesar plan to visit the capitol tomorrow?"

Casca confirmed that he did.

They bid each other goodnight and parted for bed. Before Casca blew out the lamps, Cassius came in through the open doors. "Why are your doors and windows open on such a stormy night?" he asked.

Casca replied, "Well, why are you roaming outside in this bad weather?"

“I am a brave man, Casca! I can stand bare-chested on the spot where lightning falls.”

“Men should fear the Almighty! You must not tempt the heavens.”

“I think gods make the skies thunderous to convey something to people. It is an omen for a man who has become too ambitious and proud. Something is about to happen to him!”

Casca raised a brow. "Are you talking about Caesar?"

Cassius simply replied, "Let the right person be given awards and the wrong person be given punishments!"

"The senators have planned to crown Caesar tomorrow. He will wear the crown everywhere on land and sea, except in Italy."

"I will never bow to his tyranny. I would rather commit suicide than be his slave. He cannot dominate me," said Cassius, defiantly.

Casca pushed Cassius to reveal what he really thought of Caesar. Cassius said angrily, "The Romans will easily fall prey to Caesar's tyranny. Rome will become a hopeless place. I think Caesar should be killed. I am armed now, and I don't care what danger comes my way."

Casca was thrilled. "Cassius, if you wish to right these wrongs too, say no more! Let's shake hands."

Cassius shook Casca's hand, and said, "The noblest Romans have joined hands with me on this dangerous mission. We are meeting tonight."

Cassius' friend Cinna walked in and interrupted their conversation. As soon as Casca saw Cinna, he made to leave the room. Cassius assured Casca that Cinna was a fellow conspirator.

"I have been looking for you everywhere. We need to sway Brutus to our side!" declared Cinna. Cassius handed over some letters to Cinna, and said, "Don't worry. Take these letters and toss them in through Brutus's window. Make sure he sees them." Cinna took the letters and left with a wicked glint in his eye. Cassius asked Casca to accompany him to Brutus's place.

Meanwhile, Brutus was sitting alone in his study thinking about his next course of action. "I think the only way to prevent my country from damage is to kill Caesar. If he is crowned tomorrow, he will become a threat to us. I don't have any personal motives to kill him, but I must to do it for Rome!"

Brutus's servant Lucius knocked on the door. He handed a letter to Brutus.

Brutus asked, "Lucius, is it the fifteenth of March?"

"I don't know, sir."

Brutus asked him to confirm if the fifteenth of March had arrived yet and dismissed him. He opened the letter and started reading, "Brutus, wake up and be alert. You must protect Rome and fix what's going wrong."

Lucius came back and announced that it was indeed the fifteenth day of March. Suddenly, they heard a knock on the door. Lucius left to check who it was and came back with the news that Cassius was waiting for him.

"Is Cassius alone?" asked Brutus.

"No, sir. He is here with some people."

Brutus asked for them to be let in. Cassius walked into his chamber followed by all the conspirators.

"Good morning, Brutus," Cassius greeted him. "I apologise for interrupting your sleep before the break of dawn."

Brutus replied, "It's okay. I have been awake all night. Who are these men?"

Cassius introduced all the conspirators to him one by one. Then he said, "Brutus, can I have a word with you alone?"

Brutus moved closer to Cassius's chair and they began talking in hushed tones. Meanwhile, Decius, Casca, and

Cinna pleasantly discussed the weather. After a while, Brutus and Cassius stood up and asked the conspirators to join hands with them.

Cassius said, "Let's all swear to keep our resolution!"

The conspirators vowed to protect Rome from Caesar's tyranny. After taking the oath, Cassius said, "Do you think that we should include Cicero in our plan?"

Casca, Cinna, and Metellus were in support of the idea. But Brutus was not. Cassius immediately agreed with Brutus and decided to leave Cicero out of the plan.

Decius said, "Don't you think that we should kill Mark Antony along with Caesar? Antony is the closest friend of Caesar's!"

Cassius agreed with Decius, but Brutus disagreed. "I think Mark Antony is harmless. Besides, our hands will be stained with the blood of two men. I want us to kill Caesar but only for the sake of duty. Remember, we aren't killing him for personal gain. Our deeds are for the country. And as far as Antony is concerned, we should spare him. After Caesar's demise, Antony will no longer be powerful."

Brutus's words had convinced everyone. The clock struck three, and they decided to meet at eight in the morning to execute the plan. Before leaving, Cassius expressed his doubts, "I am not sure if Caesar will come out into the public today. Unlike earlier, Caesar has become superstitious lately. He might not even venture out of his house today."

Decius assured Cassius that he would convince Caesar to visit the capitol.

Everyone stood up to leave, and Brutus said, "Gentlemen, put on your best faces when we meet next. Carry yourself with confidence like the good Roman actors do, and behave cheerfully. Good day to all of you!"

"I don't think it's a physical sickness. I think, Brutus, your mind is sick."

When they left, Brutus's wife Portia entered the room. She had been waiting for the strange men to leave.

Brutus asked, concerned, "Portia, what are you doing here? Are you ill?"

Portia replied, "No, dear. I am perfectly fine, but you don't seem to be in your senses these days. Being awake all night is bad for your health. You don't eat or sleep properly. I don't want to goad you, but I am worried about you. Tell me, what's bothering you?"

Brutus answered, "I am not feeling well, Portia."

"If you are sick, then you should stay at home and rest in your warm bed. I don't think it's a physical sickness. I think, Brutus, your mind is sick."

Portia kneeled in front of Brutus. "By all the vows you made to me during our wedding, tell me, why is your mind troubled? Why did those men visit you?"

Brutus bent towards her and picked her up. "As your wife, am I not entitled to know your troubles? Am I a limited part of you? If you can't tell me your troubles, then I'm not worthy of being your wife!" She started crying.

Brutus sighed, "My love, you are worth more than you can ever imagine. Please don't misunderstand me."

"If you love me, then I am strong enough to know your secrets. You can tell me whatever it is. I can keep a secret," she insisted.

Suddenly, they heard someone knocking on the door. Brutus requested Portia to go back inside and asked Lucius to check who was at the door. After a few moments, Lucius came back with Ligarius, a Roman soldier. Brutus stood up and hugged him.

Ligarius feebly said, "Good morning, dear Brutus."

Brutus noticed Ligarius' pale face and weak stature. "You seem sick, Ligarius. I wish you weren't sick today. I had a risky task in mind for you, had you been in good health."

Ligarius assured Brutus that he was feeling better and would gladly carry out the task for him. Brutus asked Ligarius to follow him while he explained his mission.

"Let's walk with an energetic heart, Brutus! I am satisfied that you are leading me," said Ligarius.

They started walking towards the capitol while Brutus said, "Ligarius, we have decided to put an end to the tyranny of Caesar. We will kill Julius Caesar—today!"

All of a sudden, thunder shook the sky. To Brutus, it felt like the gods were agreeing with his decision, and he walked with purpose with Ligarius by his side.

On the other hand, at Caesar's palace, both Calphurnia and Caesar hadn't slept all night. They heard the thunder in the sky rumbling all night and were worried that it was a bad omen. Calphurnia had even dreamt about Caesar's death the night before. Worried about the omens, Caesar asked his servants to tell the priests to perform a sacrifice to the gods.

Calphurnia saw Caesar getting ready and stood in his way. "Where are you going?"

Caesar replied, "I like to confront my fears, so I am going

outside right now."

Calphurnia grabbed Caesar's arm. "Please don't go anywhere today. I am scared of these omens; first I had that dream, and now, the sky is booming. The sky always announces the death of someone important. I beg you. Don't go."

"One can't avoid God's will, Calphurnia. But I don't want to worry you. So I will send Mark Antony to inform the senators that I'm not coming today."

Just then, Decius arrived to escort Caesar. “Good morning, worthy Caesar! I am here to take you to the capitol.”

“Decius, it’s good that you came! Please go to the senators and tell them that I am not coming today. It’s not that I can’t; simply tell them that I won’t.”

Decius was reluctant to go to the senators without a justification for Caesar’s absence.

"I will not make up an excuse, I am a respectable man. But, here is the real reason,” Caesar told Decius that Calphurnia had had a dream about his death and had begged him not to leave.

Decius said, “But sir, the dream has been misinterpreted! It was a lucky vision. She saw the Romans bathing in your blood, which means that you will give the blood that sustains the people of Rome. Your holy blood makes Rome pure.”

Caesar was pleased to hear Decius's interpretation. He immediately decided to leave for the capitol.

Decius reasoned that the senators had decided to offer the crown to Caesar that day, and if he didn't go, they might change their decision. Caesar relented, "Well, there is no doubt in my mind then. I am ashamed that I yielded to Calphurnia's foolish superstitions. Fetch my robe. I must get ready now!"

Publius, Brutus, Ligarius, Metellus, Casca, and the other conspirators came to accompany Caesar to the capitol.

Brutus reminded Caesar that the clock had struck eight and it was time to leave. As they made to leave, Mark Antony arrived.

Caesar greeted him, "Antony is here too! Good morning, Antony." Antony bowed and greeted Caesar. Caesar asked his servants to serve wine to everyone.

"It aches my heart to see Caesar treating us like his closest friends!" thought Brutus.

After having a glass of wine, they all left for the capitol.

Meanwhile, the priest Artemidorus was writing a letter to Caesar. He stood on the street and went over his letter one last time, "Dear Caesar, beware of Brutus. Watch Cassius closely and don't go near Casca. Caius Ligarius feels wronged by you. All these men intend to betray you and kill you. I pray to the Almighty to defend you from them. Your true friend, Artemidorus."

He decided to wait for Caesar to cross his path so he could give him the letter.

On the other hand, Portia was getting more and more worried about Brutus. She ordered Lucius to go to the senate house and come back with information about the happenings there.

Lucius asked, “But madam, for what reason should I go to the senate house?”

Portia replied, “Just go there and check if your master looks well. Also, pay close attention to the men around him.” Suddenly, she heard a scuffling sound.

She saw the fortune-teller lingering in the street not very far from her home. "Come here, you! Why are you standing there?"

The fortune-teller came forward and said, "Madam, I am waiting here for Caesar. I have a plea for him."

"Do you think that someone intends to harm Caesar?" asked Portia.

"I am not sure about that, but I am afraid for him. I wish to warn him to watch his back. Well, should go and wait for Caesar to arrive." Saying so, he walked away.

"I wish to warn him to watch his back."

Portia thought, "I must also go inside. May the gods protect my husband!"

She ordered Lucius to rush to the senators' house and return with information.

An hour later, the fortune-teller saw Caesar, his servants, and the conspirators marching down the street. A crowd of people approached Caesar's carriage and he asked his

servant to halt.
Caesar addressed the fortune-teller, "Good morning. Today is the fifteenth of March."

The fortune-teller replied, "Yes sir, but it has not passed yet."

Artemidorus pushed through the crowd and thrust the letter at Caesar. "Please read my petition first, sir. It is of great concern to you."

Caesar took the letter but kept it aside. Artemidorus said, "Caesar, please read the letter right now. It's important."

Publius scolded Artemidorus for interrupting them. Cassius added, "Artemidorus, if you want to press your petition, then present it at the capitol."

They moved past him and resumed their journey to the capitol. Soon, they reached the senate house. Caesar went inside to meet the senators. Meanwhile, the conspirators gave each other meaningful looks, confirming their plan. One of the servants wished Cassius good luck for their plan. Cassius was alarmed, wondering if the servants had caught wind of their conspiracy. He asked, "Which plan, Popillus?"

Popillus replied, "The plan to crown Caesar the king!"

Soon, Caesar stood on the platform and addressed the people of Rome. "My dear countrymen, I thank you all for crowning me as your king. I will address your problems from today itself and try to solve all of them. So please step forward with your grievances."

Cassius asked Metellus to walk up to the platform and put his plea in front of Caesar. Metellus slowly walked up the stairs and bowed to Caesar.

Metellus said, "Most mighty Caesar, I kneel before you with a humble heart. I appeal to you to repeal my brother's banishment. Please accept my request."

Caesar replied, "Don't plead for your brother, Metellus. I cannot accept your appeal."

Brutus came forward and kissed Caesar's hand. He said, "I kiss your hand, not in flattery but to put my appeal in front of you. Please repeal Publius Cimber's banishment."

Cassius also bent on one knee and pleaded, "Please Caesar, restore Publius Cimber's citizenship. I beseech you."

Caesar was shocked to see Brutus and Cassius begging for Publius' honour. At last, Caesar said firmly, "I would be convinced if I were similar to you. But I am immovable like the Northern Star. Only one star sticks to its position amongst the countless other stars in the sky. I am that star. My decision is irrevocable."

Decius also kneeled and said, “Great Caesar, please accept my appeal!”

Caesar replied, “Don’t flatter or kneel before me. It won’t work. Publius is banished and will never regain his citizenship. It’s my final decision.”

Casca was standing behind Caesar while the other conspirators were now surrounding him. Casca thought, "Enough now! Caesar won't pay heed to anyone. Now, I will let my hands speak for me."

He pulled out a dagger and stabbed Caesar. For a moment, the entire assembly stood still. Caesar slowly turned to see the owner of the dagger. He saw Casca standing behind him, holding a dagger in his hands, looking ferocious. The other conspirators followed suit and plunged their daggers into Caesar. Caesar looked into Casca's eyes, and without uttering a word crumpled like a broken leaf. Brutus grabbed the falling Caesar ... and stabbed him in the chest. Caesar looked at Brutus with wide, betrayed eyes, and before taking his last breath, he said, "You too, honourable Brutus?"

Cinna screamed, "Liberty! The tyrant is dead!"

Suddenly all hell broke loose. People started running in different directions.

Brutus gathered the courage to speak to the panicked crowd. "Senators and people, don't run away. We will not harm any of you. It was only Caesar who had to die for his pride and ambition."

Cassius began chanting, "Freedom, liberty, democracy! Brutus, go to the platform and justify our deed to the Romans."

Brutus tossed away his dagger and walked towards the platform. Meanwhile, Metellus tried to control the crowd and asked everyone to stay close in case Caesar's friends tried to take revenge.

Metellus tried to push Publius out of harm's way, but he was too stunned to move. Cassius called Trebonius and asked him Mark Antony's whereabouts. Trebonius told him that Antony had rushed home in fear.

Suddenly, they heard Brutus's voice. "Countrymen, don't be afraid. We all enter the world with our fates already sealed. At one point or another, we all have to die."

Cassius shouted, "True! We spend half our lives thinking about how we will die."

Brutus continued, "Well, we have proven to be the truest friends of Caesar. We saved him at least two decades of worry."

"Well, we have proven to be the truest friends of Caesar."

Brutus looked at Caesar's vacant face and bellowed, "Look! How peacefully our ambitious Caesar lies at the foot of Pompey's statue, as worthless as dust."

Cassius joined him. "Yes. Our names will be glorified in history for saving Rome from tyranny! Let us leave, and let Brutus lead the way. Let us follow him with the bravest of hearts!"

Brutus was stepping down from the platform to leave when he saw Antony's servant approaching him.

The servant relayed his message, "Sir, my master asks if it is safe to come here, and he promises that if he finds your explanation for killing Caesar acceptable, he will follow you through anything."

Brutus replied, "Your master is a wise and honourable man. He shall leave unharmed, it's my promise."

The servant bowed and left. Cassius expressed his suspicion about Antony. "Antony loves Caesar truly. I am not sure if he will be on our side."

Brutus said, "Don't worry Cassius, Antony will surely realise what's right."

In a few minutes, Antony arrived there with a heavy heart. As soon as he reached Caesar's corpse, he fell at his feet and started crying loudly. All the conspirators stood there, shamelessly watching Antony cry for his dearest friend.

After his tears subsided, he said wretchedly, "Dear Brutus, can you please stab me with your knife?"

Brutus replied, "Antony, I might look like a killer to you right now, but I have a pure heart. Please give me some time to explain our actions. Even I feel pity for Caesar, but this was necessary."

"Sir, I would love to be stabbed by the leaders of this era. I would rather die near my sweet friend Caesar than anywhere else. Please kill me," said Antony.

"Let me calm the masses, then I will explain everything properly," said Brutus.

Antony got up and shook hands with all the conspirators one by one. Then he said, "Now that I have shaken hands with you, you might think of me as a flatterer or a coward." He looked towards Caesar's corpse and folded his hands in apology. "I am sure that my dearest friend Caesar's soul is questioning my credibility. Forgive me, dear Caesar!"

He turned towards Brutus and Cassius, and said, "I would like for us to make an agreement."

Cassius asked, "What kind of agreement? Do we consider you as an enemy or a friend?"

"I just shook hands with you. You can consider me as a friend. But you must reveal your reasons for killing Caesar, and you must allow me to carry my friend's body to the marketplace and give a speech at his funeral."

"I permit you to give a speech in honour of your friend, Mark Antony," said Brutus.

Cassius pulled Brutus aside and said, "Do you even know what you are doing? Mark Antony is a great orator and can influence people easily."

Brutus turned to Antony, "You can give a speech on one condition. I will explain the reasons for Caesar's death to the audience before your speech. You will tell everyone that you are giving the speech with our permission. You won't say anything against us."

> Mark Antony is a great orator and can influence people easily.

Antony agreed. Soon, all the conspirators left for the marketplace, leaving Antony alone with Caesar's body. At that moment, Caesar's son Octavius' servant rode in on his horse. He was shocked to see Caesar dead and started crying. Antony consoled him and told him the whole story. He added, "Stay with me till my speech and then go to Octavius and tell him everything that has happened."

The servant agreed and helped Antony carry Caesar's corpse to the marketplace.

As soon as Cassius saw Antony and Octavius arriving, he asked Brutus to stand on the platform and begin his speech.

Brutus began in a compelling voice, "Countrymen and friends, I know you have many questions for us. But before that, I pray, please don't judge my love for Caesar. I always loved Caesar but not more than my country. I didn't want my country to become a slave to Caesar's ambitions. I killed him not for his prosperity but for his ambition. Is there anyone here who believes otherwise?"

The plebeians listened to Brutus intently. "Did I offend anyone here by killing Caesar?"

"No, Brutus!" half the crowd screamed.

Brutus continued, "Remember, my friends, I would not refrain from killing myself for my country if needed!" Now they all cheered for him.

Mark Antony climbed onto the platform with Caesar's body. Brutus requested the audience to wait for Antony's speech, and left the marketplace. There was a restless murmur rippling through the crowd.

Antony waited for a hush to fall over them. Then he began slowly, "Romans, countrymen, and friends, can I have your attention? I am not here to praise Caesar. I am

here to bury him and say a few words about him. Usually, a dead person is remembered for his evil deeds rather than his good deeds. With the permission of the most honourable men, I stand here to speak about my dearest friend, Julius Caesar. Our honourable Brutus told us that Caesar was an ambitious person. But don't you remember when Caesar brought captives to Rome who made us rich? Have you forgotten the times when Caesar sobbed for the poor? Don't you think crying for the poor is much too sober an act for an ambitious man? And friends, don't ambitious men accept the crown as soon as it's offered to them? I believe you all saw Caesar denying the crown thrice when it was offered to him. But, if Brutus says that Caesar was ambitious, then it must be true, as Brutus is an honourable man. Honourable men don't lie. But if you once loved Caesar, what's stopping you from mourning his death today?"

His voice cracked with emotion. "My heart rests with Caesar in his coffin. Please pardon me for weeping."

Meanwhile, the plebeians started whispering amongst themselves.

Antony wiped his tears and continued, "Only yesterday, Caesar's order would have been the final word, and

> Don't you think crying for the poor is much too sober an act for an ambitious man?

today, no one weeps for his death. I don't mean to stir a rebellion because I don't want to disrespect honourable Brutus and Cassius. However, today, I found Caesar's will in his room. If I read it to you, it would make you feel guilty for not respecting him. Your emotions would be stirred, and you would fight to receive even a single lock of his hair as a keepsake."

One of the plebeians shouted, "We want to hear the will! Read the will."

The other plebeians seconded him, "The will! The will!"

Antony shook his head, "No, my friends, I cannot read Caesar's will to you. The contents of his will would enrage you. I don't want to disrespect the honourable men."

The plebeians continued shouting, "The will! The will!"

Antony finally agreed to read out the will. He asked the plebeians to let him stand amidst them while reading the testament and the plebeians quickly made room for him. Antony stood close to Caesar's body, with a cloak on his hand.

He addressed the plebeians, "Do you see this? It is the same cloak that Caesar wore when the conspirators' daggers passed through his body. That's when Caesar realised the ingratitude of his closest friend Brutus.

How he loved Brutus! Oh! Poor Caesar!"

The plebeians looked at the blood-soaked cloth sadly. Some of them started crying.

Antony continued, "Don't go against the honourable men, my friends. They are wise and worthy, but I don't know what personal reasons they had for killing Caesar. Nevertheless, let me read Caesar's will to you."

He took the parchment from his servant and read aloud, "'I give seventy-five drachmas to each citizen of Rome. I leave all my private gardens, walkways, and orchards to my countrymen.'"

All the plebeians started mourning Caesar's demise. Antony cried, "There won't be another Caesar in our lives ever again. It's a big loss for us!"

One of the plebeians said, "Let's burn his body in the holy place and then use that fire to burn the traitors!"

They carried the corpse to the graveyard, leaving Antony alone. Meanwhile, Octavius's servant came and informed Antony that his master and Lepidus were waiting for him at Caesar's residence.

He also informed Antony that Cassius and Brutus had managed to escape from Rome. Antony kept Caesar's will in his robes and walked towards Caesar's palace to meet Octavius. He found Octavius and Lepidus waiting for him. He greeted them and handed them a list of the conspirators. He informed Lepidus that his brother was also involved in the conspiracy and thus would be killed. Lepidus agreed with Antony's decision without a second thought. Antony then sent Lepidus on an errand. As soon as he was gone, Octavius asked Antony why he'd included Lepidus in their plans.

> "Besides, I can control both my horse and Lepidus."

Antony explained, "Octavius, I am wiser than you. Lepidus will eventually take the blame for our deeds. Including him in our plan is a great strategy."

Octavius was not convinced. "Well, do whatever you feel is right. But, let me tell you, Lepidus is an honourable and courageous soldier," he said.

"So is my horse. Besides, I can control both my horse and Lepidus."

Antony asked Octavius to leave Lepidus's matter to him and concentrate on more important issues. "Let's organise a council and discuss the safest way to confront the conspirators. Brutus and Cassius must be raising their armies. We must also gather our armies. But first, we have to find the conspirators' secrets."

Octavius replied, "I am afraid; but let's proceed with our battle plans."

They left Caesar's palace to build their army camps.

Meanwhile, Brutus was waiting at his camp with his servants, Lucius and Lucillius. Cassius's attendant Pindarus came there to greet him on his master's behalf.

Brutus observed, "Noble Pindarus, your master seems to be displeased with me. He is acting formally with me, like an acquaintance." Pindarus didn't bother denying his suspicion.

Brutus was now worried about his weakening ties with Cassius. Suddenly, he heard the sound of soldiers marching outside his tent. He came out of the tent and saw Cassius approaching.

"You have done me wrong, my friend! I am disappointed in you," said Cassius, viciously.

Brutus was affronted. "My gods know that I have never hurt anyone. How can I hurt my closest friend?"

Cassius replied, "Brutus, you always wear a mask of sober expression—"

"Dear Cassius, please calm down. As friends, we must not discuss our grievances in front of the armies. Come, let's talk in my tent."

Cassius asked his army to retreat and the two men entered Brutus's tent.

"Here's the deal," said Cassius, "you humiliated Lucius Pella for taking bribes from the Sardinians, and when I asked you to be merciful to him you ignored my request."

"My friend, I simply did what was just. In fact, you shouldn't support such a man," said Brutus.

"Brutus, don't teach me lessons of justice and injustice. I am a senior soldier and more experienced than you. Don't you dare question me!"

"Just leave, whoever you are! You cannot be my thoughtful friend Cassius!" Brutus shouted at him.

Cassius thundered back, "Don't talk to me like that! If you care about yourself, then don't provoke me any further. I didn't know that a devil hides behind your innocent face, Brutus!"

"Yes, it is a devil! I am not one of your poor servants, Cassius.

I am an honourable soldier, and I will not listen to your rash orders. You call yourself a better soldier? Why don't you prove it on the battleground?"

"You have betrayed me in every way. If Caesar were alive, he wouldn't dare say these things to me! How dare you take me for granted!"

"I am not scared of you, Cassius. I am honest, and you know it. I would rather spill my own blood than exploit poor peasants to gain extra pennies. You have betrayed me. I asked you for some gold to gift to my soldiers, and you refused."

Cassius was bewildered. "But I never refused you any gold! The man who delivered my message was a fool. He gave you the wrong message. You always exaggerate my weaknesses, Brutus. I am disappointed."

"I don't until they start affecting me!" There was dead silence for a few minutes.

Cassius shook his head with sadness. "Brutus, you don't respect me."

"I've always loved you, I just never liked your faults," replied Brutus.

"You choose to focus on them alone!" cried Cassius. "Oh Brutus! You have become my enemy, just like Octavius and Antony." He pulled out his dagger and said, "Come, take this dagger and stab me like you stabbed Caesar! I know that even though you hated him, you loved him more than you ever loved me."

Brutus pushed his hand away, "Put your dagger away. I become rude when I am angry, and I believe you are the same. But I love and respect you more than anyone else."

Cassius and Brutus sized each other up and then finally shook hands. They asked their servants to set up their tents for the night and serve some wine.

Brutus said quietly, "Cassius, please don't mind my bad temper. I have my own sorrows. My Portia ... is dead."

"Oh dear!" Cassius gasped. "What a terrible loss! How did this happen?"

"She was worried. Someone told her that we committed Caesar's murder, and now Antony and Octavius are after me. She was full of despair. Last night, she swallowed some burning coal and took her own life."

Cassius prayed for Portia's soul.

"I can't bear to talk about this anymore. Let me drown my sorrow in wine ..." Brutus poured himself another glass.

They were a few glasses down when a messenger, Messala, arrived. Messala informed them that Antony's army had killed a hundred senators, and they were now looking for Cassius and Brutus.

"I think we should march to Philippi right now!" declared Brutus.

> We should let them waste their time and resources in reaching us while we wait here energised and well rested.

Cassius reasoned, "I think we should stay here and wait for our enemies. We should let them waste their time and resources in reaching us while we wait here, energised and well rested. We'll have a better chance of winning against them."

Brutus mulled over this for a while. "I agree with you, Cassius," he finally said. "But, the people living between here and Philippi are only loyal to us out of fear. They could easily join Antony's army on their way here to rebel against us. But if we meet our enemy in Philippi, those people would back us instead."

Cassius concurred and they decided to leave the next morning.

Cassius and his attendants left for their tents, while Brutus' entourage settled down.

Brutus insisted that they all get some rest, as they had a long and tiring day ahead of them. Long after they'd all fallen asleep, Brutus stayed awake reading a book.

When the clock struck midnight, he sensed the light of the candle dimming. The air was cold and suddenly he saw Caesar's ghost standing close to him!

He screamed, "What? Who's there? What's this vision? Please tell me what you are!"

The ghost replied, "Brutus, I am your evil spirit! I am here to tell you that you will see me at Phillipi."

Before Brutus could utter another word, the ghost vanished. Brutus yelled, "Lucius! Varras! Claudio! Wake up."

"What's wrong, sir?" Lucius tensed with his sword. Brutus told Lucius about the vision he'd seen. He asked Varras if he'd seen something in the tent. Varras replied, "No sir, I was asleep. I didn't hear or see anything. What happened?"

Brutus answered, "Nothing. Varras, you go to Cassius's tent and wake him up. Tell him that we need to proceed with our forces soon. He must be alert now. We will be leaving with our armies early in the morning."

Varras bowed and left. All the other servants left to wake up the rest of the attendants and soldiers.

In Phillipi, Antony and Octavius were ready with their forces.

Octavius gave a shout of joy, "Look! Here come our enemies! Our prayers have been answered, Antony. You said they'd stay on high grounds and lie in wait for us, but they're attacking us before we can attack them."

Antony replied, "Octavius, they want to pose as brave men. They'd much rather be somewhere else; but I can see through them."

A messenger announced that Brutus's army was approaching. Antony ordered Octavius to direct his army towards the left while Antony's army would stand on the right. But Octavius decided to take his army to the right, leaving Antony perplexed. But, he decided, this was not the time for arguments.

Within a few minutes, Brutus and Cassius marched in with their armies. However, they wanted to have a civil conversation before meeting with their enemies in the battlefield. On the other hand, Octavius was waiting for Antony's signal to attack the enemies.

Antony asked Octavius to order his army not to move and they approached the other army.

Octavius confronted the enemies. "We prefer fighting to words, unlike you," he said.

Brutus replied serenely, "Good words are better than pointless fighting."

"Like the good words you spoke while you stabbed Caesar in the back?" demanded Antony.

Octavius intervened, "Let's not forget the reason why we are here! I'd much rather spill blood in battle than sweat whilst arguing. I will keep fighting until I take revenge for the thirty-three wounds that scarred Caesar's body, or die trying at the hands of the traitors."

"Good words are better than pointless fighting."

Brutus smirked, "Octavius Caesar, you would receive a most honourable death if you were killed by my sword."

Octavius replied, "I don't think my death is written on your hands, Brutus!"

"Leave it, Brutus. Octavius is like a grumpy schoolboy. He is not worth the honour," Cassius mocked him.

Octavius had had enough. He asked Antony to accompany him back to the battleground. Before leaving, Octavius challenged them, "Listen, traitors, if you have the courage, don't show it through your words. Meet us on the field!"

The four men parted with much aggression and vigour. Brutus called Lucillius and whispered something in his ear. Cassius called Messala to hand him a very important duty.

"Messala, do me a favour! Today is my birthday, and I need something from you. Be my witness, and when someone asks about the battle, tell them that I was forced to keep our freedoms at stake in the battle. Earlier, I never believed in omens, but now I do. While we were coming to Phillipi, I saw two eagles land on our flag. Our soldiers fed them. This morning they were gone, instead many kites, crows, and ravens flew above us like we were their prey. I am afraid that we might lose the battle."

Messala reassured Cassius and advised him to go back to not believing in omens. Before they could discuss it any further, Brutus returned with Lucillius. Cassius laid a hand on Brutus' shoulder. "Brutus, the gods have been merciful to us today. I don't want to dwell on the possibilities, but I always prepare myself for the worst.

Tell me, Brutus, what would you do if we lost the battle?"

Brutus replied, "I would remain patient and calm. I would submit to whatever the gods have decided for me. But I won't commit suicide; it is a most cowardly act."

"And what would you do if you were chained up and dragged through the streets of Rome by your enemies?"

"I will never allow anyone to drag me in chains. But today, our mission will come to an end. What we began on the fifteenth of March ends today. This might be our last meeting, but if we meet again, we will smile and shake hands like old friends. For now, I say farewell to you, my dearest friend and brother."

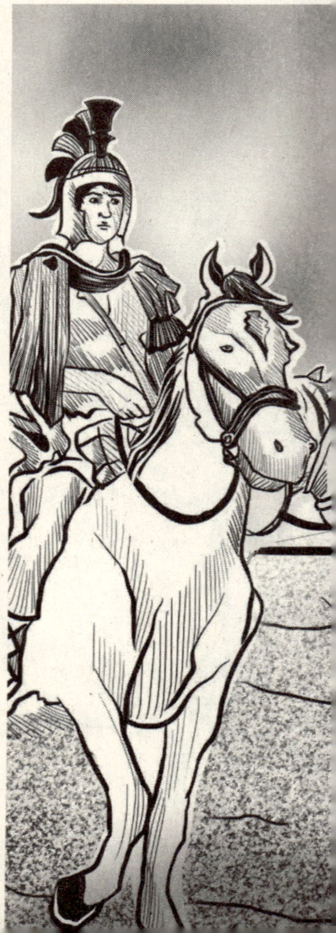

Cassius smiled at him, "Farewell, dear Brutus! We'll surely smile and shake hands if we meet again. If not, then this is a great goodbye."

"Come, let's meet our destinies

in the battleground."

When they reached the field, they were greeted by hordes of their enemies, waiting to pounce on them.

Both Brutus and Cassius were alarmed to see such a large army. However, they gathered their courage and directed their troops to effectively attack the enemy.

Brutus shouted, "Messala, ride on your horse. Ride fast! Give my orders to Cassius' troops!"

The battlefield was filled with deafening sounds of clinking swords and desperate screams. Brutus stood in the thick of it, watching, observing the destruction around him.

> "My soldiers are dying, and some of them have fled already. Cowards! Now I'm their enemy."

He noticed that Octavius's soldiers were weakening. He immediately shouted, "Messala, Octavius's army is fainthearted right now. This is the right time to attack them. Tell Cassius' army to attack now!"

Messala followed his master's orders and rode in Cassius' direction. Soon, Cassius and Titinius descended on the field. They stood on the outskirts of the field and watched the battle closely.

Cassius said anxiously, "Titinius, my soldiers are dying,

and some of them have fled already. Cowards! Now I'm their enemy."

"Brutus should've been more patient. While he had an advantage, we got outnumbered by Antony's men!" said Titinius.

Pindarus came running and screamed at Cassius to retreat his army. "Sir, Mark Antony has taken over our camp! You should run as far from here as possible."

"I am far away enough already!" Cassius looked hard at his camp. "Are our tents on fire?"

Titinius nodded gravely. Cassius was now enraged. He urged Titinius to get on his horse quickly and get as close to the camp as possible, to find out if the troops were their friends or enemies. Titinius promised to return within the blink of an eye and rode off.

Meanwhile, Cassius asked Pindarus to climb the hill and keep an eye on Titinius and the battlefield. Pindarus ascended the hill and stood at the summit to get a clear view of the battlefield and their comrade Titinius.

Cassius couldn't help thinking, "Today was the day when I first breathed and today might be the day that I breathe for the last time. My life has come full circle."

He called out to Pindarus, "What do you see, my boy?"

Pindarus screamed in shock.

"What's happening?"

Pindarus shouted, "Sir, I see horsemen surrounding poor Titinius. He is trying to fight each one of them courageously. Oh no! Now they have dismounted. So has he ... He's been taken prisoner!"

Suddenly, they heard a loud scream. The two men concluded that the soldiers who'd surrounded Titinius had perhaps killed him and were shouting for victory. Cassius softly asked Pindarus to stop watching the massacre.

"I am a coward to have waited long enough to see my best friend die," he said grimly. "Come, Pindarus, I have an important task for you. Do you remember when I rescued you from Parthia and took you as a prisoner?"

Pindarus nodded. Cassius continued, "I spared you and

made you promise to do whatever I asked for in the future. This is the moment to fulfil your oath, Pindarus."

Cassius pulled out his dagger and offered it to Pindarus. "Stab me with this dagger, and you shall be free forever. This is the weapon that scarred Caesar's body, and I want the same dagger to run through my chest. Don't hesitate Pindarus, kill me!"

Pindarus obediently took the sword, his hands shaking, and stabbed Cassius. Cassius collapsed and painfully uttered his final words, "Finally, you are avenged Caesar!"

Pindarus watched the light dimming in his master's eyes. "I am free now. But I never wanted to be free this way. If I do as I please I won't remain free for much longer. I will run to another country where no Romans can find me."

Saying this, he rode past the hills and miles away. In the meantime, Titinius and Messala were riding up the hill with some good news. Messala said, "We'll give Cassius a surprise! He will be happy to know that Brutus's forces overthrew Octavius's forces."

Titinius replied, "Oh yes, it will definitely comfort him."

They came to a standstill at the hilltop. "Titinius, why is this place so quiet? Where are Cassius and Pindarus?"

"I left them right here. I don't know where they went!"

Suddenly, Messala spotted a body lying behind a rock.

"Is that—is that Cassius? Oh no!"

Titinius cried, "How did this happen? The possibility of losing the battle must have driven him to end his own life! Oh! I wish I had returned sooner."

Messala sobbed, "Yes, he killed himself. Why does despair and doubt drive men to such grave lengths?"

No words were spoken for a few minutes. The two men were shocked out of reason.

Finally, Titinius looked around for Pindarus. Messala said with a heavy heart, "You continue looking for Pindarus, I will go deliver this devastating news to Brutus. Although I know he'd much rather stick knives in his ears than listen to this."

"They placed the wreath of victory on my head to pass it on to you."

While Messala was gone, Titinius wept over his friend's body. "Oh brave Cassius! Why did you send me away? Why didn't you wait for my return? Did you misunderstood the shouts? They placed the wreath of victory on my head to pass it on to you."

He bowed and placed the wreath on Cassius's head. "This is what Brutus would have wanted."

Titinius picked up Cassius's dagger and stabbed himself in the heart.

Brutus, Messala and the other attendants arrived at the hilltop. The sight that greeted them left them shaken.

Cassius and Titinius lay beside each other, covered in blood, unmoving.

"Oh Julius Caesar! You remain strong as ever. Your ghost is driving us to kill ourselves!" Brutus moaned.

Cato pointed to Cassius's crown. "Sweet Titinius, he put the crown of victory on Cassius' head before dying."

Brutus' voice quivered as he said, "I have never met Romans as good as these two. We must conduct their funerals properly. Take their bodies to the island of Thasos. We cannot hold the funeral at our camp, our men will lose all hope. For now, we must all proceed to the battlefield and prepare for the second battle."

A few servants carefully picked up the bodies, and the rest of them followed Brutus and Messala to the battlefield.

On the battlefield, they were met with a grave sight. Brutus' army was losing miserably. They were surrounded on all sides and rapidly losing morale.

Brutus spurred his army on, "Come on, soldiers! Keep your heads up and fight for your country."

Brutus, Messala, and Flavio went in separate directions to instruct their soldiers.

Cato bellowed, "I am Cato, son of the great Marcus Cato. I am an enemy of the tyrants. If anyone here has the courage, then come and fight me!"

Cato's proclamation gave Lucillius a brilliant idea. He yelled, "For anyone who is listening, I am Brutus, Marcus Brutus! Our country's friend, Marcus Brutus!"

Before Lucillius' distraction could work, young Cato was killed. Lucillius quickly dropped his defence and ran to where Cato lay motionless.

Lucillius dropped next to Cato's body, eyes full of tears. "My friend Cato, so young and noble; now slain. Your death was as brave as Titinius's death. You will be honoured!"

Suddenly he felt the tip of a sword against his neck. A soldier of Antony's said, "Surrender! Or you will die!"

"I prefer dying! Take this money and kill me right now. You would be honoured to kill the great Brutus," said Lucillius.

Another soldier stopped him, "Wait! He is a noble prisoner. We must not kill him. Here comes the general. My lord, we captured Brutus!"

Antony looked around perplexed. "Where is Brutus?" He spotted Lucillius. "Your prisoner is not Brutus; that is Lucillius!"

Lucillius sneered, "Brutus is safe, Antony. No enemy can capture the honourable Brutus because the gods themselves protect him."

Antony didn't answer Lucillius. He turned to his soldiers and said, "He may not be Brutus, but this man is a valuable possession. Be gentle with him and keep him happy; I'd rather have him as a friend. Go ahead, and find out if Brutus is alive."

The soldiers followed Antony's orders and left with Lucillius in tow. Antony rode off to meet Octavius.

On the other side of the battlefield, Brutus was resting on a rock with his attendants, bloody and sweaty. One of the attendants asked, "Sir, how many soldiers are remaining in the battle?"

Brutus replied, "I suppose we are the last few men remaining. Clitus, can you do me a favour?"

He whispered something in Clitus's ears. Clitus immediately refused. Brutus approached other servants, but they all refused to carry out his orders. Soon, the servants realised he'd asked them all the same thing.

At last, Brutus called Volumnius. "Volumnius, I am being terrorised by Caesar's ghost. I know that my time has come. I must die."

Volumnius said firmly, "No sir, it has not."

Brutus smiled sadly, "I am sure it has, Volumnius. You understand the ways of the world. Our enemies have cornered us to our graves."

The sounds coming from the battlefield grew stronger. Brutus said decisively, "It is nobler to jump into my grave than be pushed in by my enemies.

Volumnius, we've grown up together. For the sake of our friendship, I plead you to take my sword and stab me with it."

Volumnius replied, "My lord, being a good friend, I can't." The sounds from the battlefield were now deafening. Clitus panicked and said, "My lord, we can't stay here. We must leave!"

"My countrymen and friends," said Brutus, "I bid farewell to you. My heart swells when I look at you. You have all served me with honesty and loyalty. I cannot thank you enough. When my life ends today, I will get more glory than Mark Antony or Octavius. My bones feel weak now. It is time for me to rest. Farewell!"

They heard cries of "Run! Run!" coming from the field. Clitus shouted, "Run, my lord!"

But Brutus didn't move. Soon, all the attendants left except for Strato. When Strato was also about to leave, Brutus requested him, "Strato, I beg you to stay with me. You are an honourable man and I need you to do something for me."

He gave his sword to Strato, "I want you to hold my sword while I run myself into it."

They shook hands as Strato whispered, "Farewell, my lord," and held out Brutus' sword.

"Now you are at rest, Caesar," said Brutus and ran into his own sword.

Antony, Octavius and Messala rode in on their horses, the battle almost won. They came to a standstill upon seeing Brutus' corpse.

There was a sadness in the air as Antony soliloquised, "Here lies the noblest Roman of them all! The only one to have conspired for his country and not for jealousy."

"He shall have the most respectful burial," said Octavius. "Order the armies to rest. It's time to go home and bask in the glory of our victory."

"As he was valiant, I honour him.
But, as he was ambitious, I slew him."

– **Brutus**, Act III, Scene 2

Julius Caesar

Julius Caesar, also known as *The Tragedy of Julius Caesar*, is a popular tragedy written by William Shakespeare, published in 1623. The story is inspired by the real historical event of the assassination of the Roman pioneer Julius Caesar, and the civil war following his death.

Shakespeare builds a world surrounding military conquests and political intrigue. The play revolves around the themes of jealousy, power, greed and betrayal. Caesar's most trusted men conspire against him by painting him in the position of a dictator of Rome.

Shakespeare uses Roman superstitions and omens to set the background for the inevitable tragedy. In that era, occurrences like thunder, unusual weather and meteorological occurrences were regarded as indicators of future disasters.

Themes

Ambition

One of the central themes of the story of *Julius Caesar* is ambition. Brutus thought that Caesar's ambition was fatal for Rome's future, which is why he decided to put an end to it. The Romans later thought that Brutus was ambitious and greedy for the crown when he joined the conspirators in killing Caesar. In reality, the most harmful ambition was that of Cassius. He was jealous of Caesar's achievements and wished to kill him, but not bear the burden of his death. So, he convinced Brutus, Casca and many other men to join him in killing Caesar for his personal gain. His ambition led to one of the greatest tragedies of Rome.

Oratory Skills

The tragedy of Julius Caesar is the perfect example of how speech and oratorical abilities can turn events in one's favour. At the beginning of the story, the readers are told about Caesar's abilities to convince the audience merely with his words.

Later in the story, we notice more incidents where speech changes the course of events. For example, after the murder of Caesar, Brutus gives a strong speech that convinces the Romans of Caesar's ruthless ambition. However, right after Brutus's speech, Antony gives an even more persuasive speech where he is able to move the Romans emotionally and turn them in his favour.

OMENS

The Romans took their omens very seriously, in the sixteenth century and in *Julius Caesar* as well. However, Caesar himself doesn't give much importance to omens and disregards them. He does not listen to Calpurnia or the fortune-teller, who warns him about his demise beforehand. On the other hand, we see several misinterpretation of omens. For example, Casca interprets coincidental happenings like owls screeching during the day or a man with a burning hand as the universe's warning of Caesar's wish to rule and destroy Rome in the original play.

Answer me!

Q1. Who was Pompey? Why was Julius Caesar's triumph over Pompey a conflicting issue amongst the Romans?

Q2. Find out the difference between assassination, killing and murder. Which word best describes Julius Caesar's death in the story?

Q3. Describe Calpurnia's dream in your words. How did Decius Brutus interpret it?

Q4. Write a character sketch of Brutus in 250-300 words.

Q5. Write an analytical description of Antony's speech after Julius Caesar's assassination.

Q6. Do you believe in omens and superstitions? Mention the superstitions that you noticed in the story and their effect on the plot.

Q7. Why was Cassius worried about Antony's speech at the funeral? On what conditions was he finally allowed to speak?

Q8. Do you think Antony avenged his friend Caesar's murder rightly?

Q9. Why was Portia worried for Brutus?

Q10. If you were to rewrite the ending of the story, how would you end it? Also, give a new title to the story.

Q11. Read the extract given below and answer the following questions:

Caesar looked into Casca's eyes, and without uttering a

word crumpled like a broken leaf. Brutus grabbed the falling Caesar ... and stabbed him in the chest. Caesar looked at Brutus with wide, betrayed eyes, and before taking his last breath, he said, "You too, honourable Brutus?"

• Why was Caesar shocked to see Brutus as one of the conspirators?

• Why was Brutus called "honourable" by Caesar? Where else do you find Brutus being called honourable and by whom?

Q12. What were the contents of Caesar's will? How did it turn the Romans in favour of Caesar?

Q13. What did Brutus ask of Strato and why?

Q14. Write the death scene of Julius Caesar from the perspective of Brutus.

Q15. "I always loved Caesar, but not more than my country." Who said this, and does it justify Caesar's murder in your eyes?

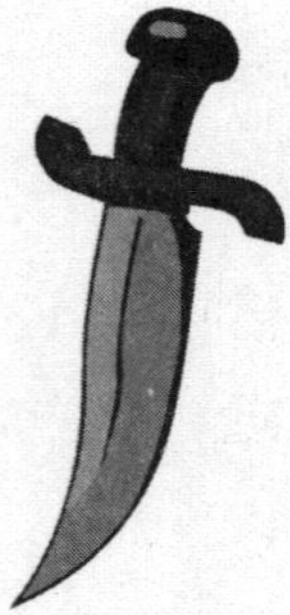

The end.